One
Step at
a Time

One Step at a Time

by
Frances Carfi Matranga
Illustrated by
Michael Hackett

Publishing House
St. Louis

Copyright © 1987 Concordia Publishing House
3558 S. Jefferson Avenue, St. Louis, MO 63118-3968
Manufactured in the United States of America

Library of Congress Cataloging-in-Publication Data

Matranga, Frances Carfi.
    One step at a time.

        (The Christian reader)
        Summary: Dottie struggles between loyalty to her troubled friend Gloria, who is always urging her to do wrong, and her own sense of doing what is morally right.
        [1. Friendship—Fiction. 2. Conduct of life—Fiction. 3. Christian life—Fiction] I. Title. II. Series.
PZ7.M43140n 1987   [Fic]   86-32646
ISBN 0-570-03642-9 (pbk.)

---

1 2 3 4 5 6 7 8 9 10   MAL   96 95 94 93 92 91 90 89 88 87

To Margaret Melrose Montague,
my dear lifelong friend

Contents

1
Rebellious Dotty

Dotty had just settled down in the family room to read, when Bruce came in. He picked up the full wastebasket and turned to look at her.

"Hey, Dot, how about taking out the rest of the trash for me? The guys are waiting to play ball and . . . "

"No!" she snapped, interrupting him. "That's your job."

The 10-year-old mumbled something as he stamped out of the room.

"And don't go calling me names!" she shouted after him. "You don't help me with my chores!"

Mrs. Russell appeared in the doorway. "Must you yell at your brother like that? Really, Dorothy!" She never called Dotty "Dorothy" unless she was annoyed with her.

"He's a pest. I did my chores, and now he wants me to help with his. If he expects to play with his friends, why doesn't he do his Saturday chores early instead of staying in bed half the morning?"

"You've got a point there, but it's no reason to shout. Is your good cotton dress ready for Sunday school tomorrow? You said it needed ironing the last time you wore it."

Dotty flung down her magazine. "Sunday school! Why do I have to go? Isn't it enough that I go to worship service? Sunday school is okay for little kids, but I'm no little kid. I'm practically 12, and I don't want to go anymore."

"Let's not start that again," her mother said in her no-nonsense voice. "Your father and I want you to go, and that's final."

"Sunday school just covers the same ol' Bible stories I've heard a million times."

"It covers more than that, Dotty; and it's helped you to memorize Scripture, hasn't it?"

"Yeah, but then I forget what I memorized, so why bother?"

"The Bible says to hide the Word of God in your heart," her mother reminded her. "You'll recall God's word when you need it. Learning Scripture is never a waste of time—and it's a good idea to review what you've memorized now and then."

"Can't I do that without going to Sunday school? Mrs. Courtney is so old-fashioned and strict," Dotty complained. "She's always telling us what good little children shouldn't do. She makes me feel as if God is spying on my every move."

"Spying? What a word to use in connection with the Lord!"

"Sorry," Dotty mumbled. "But why must she emphasize negative things? Can't do this and can't do that. I'm sick of being told what I can and can't do! You tell me. Daddy tells me. My Sunday school teacher tells me. What am I, a baby? I can think for myself!"

"Now just a minute, young lady! Have you any idea how rebellious you sound? Your father and I are simply doing our duty as parents, and I think we stress the positive more than the negative. As for Mrs. Courtney—well, she's trying to keep her

11

class on the straight and narrow path. She may not be going about it the way you or I would like, but she cares about you kids. Remember that."

"Suppose you taught Sunday school. What would you emphasize?" Dotty asked her mother.

Mrs. Russell thought for a moment. "How much Jesus loves us—that's what I'd emphasize. If youngsters truly understood the depth of Christ's love and what His sacrifice on the cross has done for us, they'd *want* to please Him with how they live their lives."

Dotty shifted in her seat, not meeting her mother's eyes. She had grown up knowing about Jesus, but it seemed to make a difference only when she was scared—such as during a bad storm, or when her favorite grandfather was killed in a car accident. Sometimes she prayed for things, but without really expecting positive results. When she went to church she enjoyed the music, but her mind wandered during the sermon. When she did pay attention, she wondered if anybody besides the preacher really thought about Jesus every day of the week. Would it make a difference if a person involved God in every little decision?

"I think I'll iron my dress now," she said, getting to her feet. "Then may I go to the mall? I like to window-shop. Could I have my allowance now, in case I want to buy something?"

"My purse is on the chair in my bedroom. Take your three dollars out of my wallet."

"Thanks, Mom."

Dotty took the bills from her mother's wallet. Seeing a number of other one-dollar bills, she wished she could take one extra. For a moment she was tempted. Her mother wouldn't know. She never kept track of exactly how much money was in her wallet, but that would be stealing.

Dotty put the wallet away and tucked her allowance into her beige shoulder-strap purse. A tenth of it would go into the offering plate tomorrow. Tithing was important, and she always gave willingly. How else would the church pay its expenses if people didn't tithe? Besides, it felt kinda good to give her tithe back to the Lord.

She was ironing her dress in the kitchen when the telephone rang.

"It's Gloria," her mother called from the living room.

Dotty took the phone from her. "Hi, Gloria. What's up?"

13

"Can you have lunch with me today and stay awhile? My mother now works from nine to one on Saturday, so I'm here alone."

"Just a minute. Mom, can I have lunch at Gloria's house? I could go straight from the shopping center."

Her mother nodded.

"I can come, Gloria. See you before noon." She hung up, glad for the invitation. Right now she wanted to go to the mall by herself, but it would be a long afternoon. Gloria could always think of something to pass the time.

Their friendship had begun six months before when one of their sixth-grade classmates deliberately tripped Gloria at recess. Dotty had helped her up and brushed her off, while scolding the culprit.

"It was an accident," he told her.

"Accident, my eye! I saw you do it. Did you hurt yourself, Gloria?"

"I'm okay, Dorothy. Thanks."

"My friends call me Dotty."

Soon after that, Gloria had invited her to her house, and they started hanging around together.

The June day was so perfect that Dotty wished it would last forever. She enjoyed ambling around the shopping mall and looking at the show-window displays, some interesting, some just junk. Dotty pretended she had a pocketful of bills. She'd buy her mother that lacy pink blouse in the window of The Stylish Dress Shop. Pink was her mother's color; it looked great against her fair skin. And how about a bunch of golf balls for her dad—the best money could buy! Golf was his favorite sport. And maybe her pesky brother would appreciate a new baseball bat. The one he had was cracked. For herself she'd get a great new pair of jeans to replace her faded ones. She had another pair at home, but she wanted the latest color.

Dotty became aware of a face smiling at her from the show window. It took a moment to recognize it as her own. She giggled, thinking, *I walk around almost in a trance when I daydream.* That was because nobody was with her to talk and break the spell. Half the time she wasn't even aware of the people around her. It was such fun to daydream. Perhaps that was why she liked to window-shop by herself.

She paused in front of the toy store. A cute

15

little girl was looking at the dolls in the window. With her big, brown eyes and curly hair, she looked like a doll herself, Dotty thought.

"Which doll do you like best?" she asked her.

"That one," the child replied, pointing.

"The baby doll? I think I like that one best, too," Dotty said. "It looks so cuddly."

"We're gonna have a *real* baby in our house," the preschooler told her with a big smile. "Before the snow comes. Mama said so. That's my mama over there." She gestured toward a young woman watching them from a bench nearby.

Dotty smiled at the mother and said to the daughter, "You'll be the big sister, won't you. You gonna help Mama take care of the baby?"

The child bobbed her head. "It'll be *my* baby, too," she said proudly.

"You bet. 'Bye now."

In Woolworth's, Dotty found an unexpected bargain in unbreakable combs—a 12-piece package of various sizes and colors for 99 cents. She couldn't resist buying a package. She then walked across the mall to The Game Room and looked in the window. A couple of boys were at the pinball machines. A redheaded boy was playing a video

16

game, while a dark-haired companion looked on. They appeared to be about 14. Dotty decided to go in and watch the video game.

"Hi, Blondie," the dark-haired boy said with a smile as she paused beside him. She smiled back.

After watching the other boy blast figures off the screen left and right, she said, "He's good, isn't he?"

"He should be. He's had plenty of practice. You like to play?"

"Yeah, but I'd rather spend my money on other things." She stood watching till the game ended.

"Well, that's it—a buck's worth," said the redhead. "Let's go, Stan."

"Maybe this chick would like to join us," Stan suggested. "What's your name, Blondie?"

"Dorothy. Join you for what?" she asked out of curiosity.

"It's a great day and we're gonna set up camp in the woods. Tent, cooking gear, the works. We're gonna roast hotdogs and marshmallows. Why don'tcha come along."

Me go into the woods with two strange boys? No sir!

2
Temperamental Gloria

"I don't think so," Dotty said.

"Aw, c'mon; be a sport." Stan grabbed her hand and gave it a squeeze. "We'll have fun together."

What kind of fun? Dotty felt like asking, but said instead, "No, thanks; and let go of me, please."

Dotty had heard a schoolmate with a 14-year-old brother remark that most boys that age were disgusting. Their main interests were dirty books and pictures of nude girls. Dotty had read the same thing in *Are You There, God? It's Me, Margaret*, by author Judy Blume. Perhaps it was true.

"C'mon, Dorothy; come to our tent," Stan insisted. "We'll show you a good time—I promise."

"I said, let go of me! Do I have to kick you?"

He dropped her hand and sprang out of range as Dotty's blue eyes flashed sparks at him. "Wow, Curtis, this one's a firecracker!"

Curtis grinned. "A firecracker in our tent would be interesting, huh? You sure you don't wanta join us, honey?"

Dotty gave him a withering look and stalked out of The Game Room without a backward glance.

There was still time before lunch. She decided to walk over to Christian Books and Gifts. She liked to look at their ceramic angels and children in attitudes of prayer. Her mother collected angel figurines, and Dotty planned to give her one for Christmas.

Already she was saving 50 cents a week out of her allowance toward Christmas presents. That and 30 cents for tithing left $2.20 for herself. It was a struggle sometimes not to spend it all at once. But then she'd have nothing for the rest of the week. She was glad Gloria had invited her for lunch today, or she'd be tempted to stop at the Pizza Parlor for a slice of pizza and a soft drink.

Gloria was an only child and received four dollars a week allowance. She seemed to have more things than Dotty, but she was generous about sharing. Just last week she'd given Dotty a brand new ballpoint pen.

Inside the Christian store, on a table near the door, Dotty saw some pretty bookmarks with floral borders. They were only 10 cents each. She bought two printed with the Lord's Prayer—one for Gloria and one for herself.

As she strolled to her friend's house beneath shady, maple trees lining the sidewalks, she thought of how pretty Sunnyville was. Well-kept yards were blooming with petunias, irises, early roses, and pink, mountain laurel. June was busting out all over!

Dotty was glad she lived in a suburb of New York City. Sometimes Dad took the family to the Bronx Zoo. She loved seeing the animals. Once her father took them to the top of the Empire State Building. What a view!

Gloria was glad to see her. So was Pixie, her golden-brown cocker spaniel, who greeted Dotty by licking her hand. The dog followed the girls into the kitchen.

"We can bake a frozen pizza for lunch," Gloria said.

"Just what I was wishing for," Dotty told her.

"And there's leftover chocolate cake. You shopped?"

"Just combs. And bookmarks—one for each of us. They're both the same." Dotty gave her one.

"Thanks. Oh, it's got the Lord's Prayer on it. I used to . . . "

Gloria didn't finish her sentence. "Used to what?" Dotty prompted.

"Oh—used to say that prayer every morning when I woke up."

"But not anymore?"

"Nope." Gloria shrugged. "Don't go to church anymore, either."

"Why not?"

"Don't feel like it, that's why."

"And your parents let you get away with it?"

"They stopped going, too!" The words snapped out with such anger that they startled Dotty. She wondered, *Was it because of my remark? Is Gloria mad at her parents? She seems touchy lately.*

21

"Uh, look—I bought a whole package of combs on sale." Dotty pulled the plastic package out of the paper bag. "Tear it open. Choose one for yourself. Take two, if you like—a big one and a small one."

Gloria's smile returned as she selected a red comb and a blue one. Then she poured some dog chow into Pixie's bowl and preheated the oven for the pizza.

While eating lunch, Dotty learned that her friend was a year older than she. "I didn't know that, being that we're in the same grade," she said. "So that's why you're taller and your chest is starting to develop? Did you flunk a grade?"

"Yeah, I did fifth grade twice when I lived in Hastings. My parents threatened summer school if I flunk again. Who wants to spend vacation time studying? School'll be out before long, Dotty, and we'll have fun."

After clearing the table, the girls went outside and sat on the porch glider. Pixie padded after them and curled up in a patch of sunshine. She was getting on in years. Dotty leaned over to stroke her head. Then she said, "I always look forward to vacation time, but after a while it gets boring, and I can't wait to go back to school."

"Stick with me and you won't be bored this summer," Gloria told her, making the glider swing. "We'll find exciting things to do."

"Like what?"

"Oh . . . we'll see." Gloria gave her a sly look and giggled.

"Gloria! Tell me!"

"Nope. Gotta get to know you better first."

"What for? What are you talking about?" Dotty poked her and got two pokes back. They giggled. "Okay, surprise me," Dotty assented. "Say, got any paper dolls?"

"There's some in my room somewhere. I'll show them to you another time. I just feel like lying around today, if you don't mind. I love this glider. Sometimes when I feel lazy and it's swinging, it puts me to sleep." Gloria pushed on the floor with her foot to keep it going. "Not that I'm gonna doze off with you here."

For something interesting to say, Dotty told her about the boys who tried to pick her up at the mall. "Do I look dumb or something? As if I'd go

23

off with a couple of strangers! To the woods yet! Now why do you s'pose they'd want to take a girl to the woods with them? Hah! You needn't answer that. Jerks!"

"My grandmother used to carry a long hat pin in her purse in case a guy got fresh with her," said Gloria. She snickered. "Not a bad idea. What else is interesting?"

Dotty searched her mind. "My father's going to build a tree house for Bruce this summer. And he might take us to the Bronx Zoo again. And he promised to paint my bicycle. And he . . ."

"I don't want to talk about fathers," Gloria interrupted.

"But I want to tell you what he . . . "

"Did you hear me!" Gloria yelled, her face getting all red.

Dotty stared at her with her mouth open. She felt as if she'd been slapped. Even the dog had raised her head to stare.

She must be mad at her dad. But she needn't take it out on me!

Gloria leaned back in the glider and closed her eyes. "Guess I *will* take a nap," she muttered, retreating into herself like an animal burrowing into the corner of its cage.

Dotty knew she was being dismissed. Feeling angry and hurt at such treatment, she rose stiffly and left.

3
Still Friends

Dotty's mind wandered more than usual during Sunday school and the worship service. She kept thinking about Gloria. When they first started hanging around together, Gloria seemed really nice. Neither girl had a best friend, and Dotty was optimistic about the two of them. But Gloria seemed different lately—temperamental, changeable. She was like one of those trick pictures that changed color as you moved it in your hand. Could it have something to do with hormones, like her teacher taught in health class, since Gloria was older than Dotty? But what did that have to do with fathers?

She had met Gloria's father, although she hadn't seen him lately. He sold insurance for a living and was out a lot. Gloria's mother worked in a stationery store. Mr. Powell was tall and blond and could have passed for a movie star, he was that handsome. Mrs. Powell, on the other hand, was a plain woman. They were like a cardinal and a little brown wren, Dotty thought. You'd never connect them if you didn't know they were married. Dotty's own father was an accountant, and her mother worked as cashier at The Martin Family Restaurant. Her parents were neither handsome nor plain—just ordinary, pleasant-looking folks.

The pastor was talking about the prophet Elijah. Dotty tried to listen, but soon her mind detoured again.

Why did Gloria lash out when I mentioned what Daddy plans to do for Bruce and me? Did it make her angry because her father's new job leaves little time for him to spend with her? Working on commission means hustling all the time to get new clients. He's hardly ever home. Maybe Gloria's jealous that my father spends time with his family.

Dotty let out a big sigh. A kid in front of her

turned around and gave her a look. It reminded her she was in church, and she lowered her head self-consciously. Her sigh must have sounded like she was bored with the sermon. Actually, she'd heard very little of it.

She still felt hurt over yesterday, but her anger was gone. She wished Gloria would confide in her instead of keeping her deepest feelings to herself. That meant she didn't consider Dotty her best friend yet. Best friends talked things over, didn't they?

Sometimes Dotty had the feeling Gloria wore a mask to hide her hurts. She put on a cheerful face, but Dotty could sense that something was bothering her. A couple of times, she had glimpsed a sad, lonely expression on her friend's face when Gloria thought no one was looking. And now these occasional outbursts of temper!

Dotty felt downcast all day. Even on Monday, while walking to school, her heart was heavy—until she heard, "Dotty! Dotty, wait up!" and turned to see Gloria running toward her. Her heartbeat quickened as she waited.

Gloria paused to catch her breath. Then she

said, "I want you to know I'm sorry about Saturday. I was mean to you, and I've been feeling bad about it. Honest, Dot, I'm sorry. Can we still be friends?"

Seeing the repentance on Gloria's face, Dotty could not doubt her sincerity. And she really did like Gloria. Nobody was perfect, after all. She nodded and smiled, and suddenly her heart felt light again.

Gloria gave a sigh of relief. "I feel better now."

"Me, too," Dotty admitted. "I was peeved at you for a while, but I'm glad we've made up."

The sun was shining through Gloria's ringlets, turning her hair into a golden halo. She was a pretty girl and looked like her father. They both had brown eyes, uncommon for blonds.

"Let's forget Saturday and start over again," Gloria said cheerfully. "Hey, there's Randy and Ken by the school door. Race you!" They giggled and started running. "You still got a crush on Randy, Dotty?"

"Hush! You want him to hear?" Dotty beat Gloria to the side entrance of Lincoln Elementary School. Randy smiled at her and held the door open for both girls.

"Thanks," Dotty said breathlessly as she walked past him into the building. Randy Wyler was just about the nicest boy in Miss Brent's sixth grade class. In the whole school, maybe. He sure was good-looking, with eyes bluer and hair blonder than her own. She could bet he'd still be a nice kid when he was 14. Not like those guys at the mall.

It turned out to be a good day all day, and after school Dotty walked Gloria home to have a look at her paper dolls. Pixie was chained to her kennel in the backyard. They stopped to pet her. She wriggled a little at the sight of them. You could tell she wanted to leap up and lick their faces, but she didn't have the strength. Dotty leaned over and kissed the top of her head. She had become very fond of the cocker spaniel.

Gloria knelt to hug her pet. "Poor Pixie. You're getting old, aren't you?" Gloria turned to Dotty. "She's watched over me since I was born. She was Mom's pet even before she got married."

"How old is Pixie?"

"Oh, she's about 15. That's really old for a dog. I can't stand to think of her dying. She's been with us forever." Gloria gave the pet another hug and

31

ran fresh water from the hose into her bowl. The other bowl still had dog chow in it.

"Here, Dotty, take my key to the back door. The paper dolls are somewhere on the bottom shelf of my bookcase. I'll be with you as soon as I walk the dog."

Ten minutes later, Gloria joined Dotty, and the girls decided to act out a game with the paper dolls. Dotty had some at home and loved designing costumes for them. The pretty clothes made playing with paper dolls enjoyable.

Selecting one with wavy, brown hair, Dotty said, "This is me, and my name is Anita. Hmm, I think I'll wear this embroidered shirt and these designer jeans."

"And this is me—Dawn." Gloria picked up a paper doll with blue eyes and short blond curls like her own. "Let's go window-shopping as soon as we get dressed, shall we, Anita? Let me see now . . . " She rummaged among the costumes. "This blouse, I think, and these slacks . . . and here's a straight loose jacket with big pockets."

"Isn't it kinda warm for a jacket?"

"I need pockets. You'd better choose something with pockets, too, Anita."

"Why, Dawn? Aren't we just going window shopping? If we're shopping for real, I'll bring a purse," Anita said.

"We're going counter shopping at Woolworth's. The pockets are for the things we pick up," Dawn said lightly.

"Pick up?"

"Yeah, Man! We're going shoplifting."

Dotty stared at her friend, forgetting they were Dawn and Anita. "You kidding, Gloria?"

Gloria grinned at her. "C'mon, Anita, let's live dangerously for a change."

"Well . . . okay." Dotty relaxed. It was just a game, but she couldn't help thinking Gloria's sense of humor was a bit weird.

4
Brat!

Dotty felt good as she walked home from Gloria's house. So far it had been a perfect day. The weather was great, wrapped in sunshine, and she and Gloria were friends again. She chuckled as she thought about the shoplifting with the paper dolls. Crazy game! And yet, it had been fun to imagine picking up anything you wanted that could fit into your pockets. Anita had lifted a necklace, a pocket calculator, a paperback novel, and a package of rubber bands. *Boy, wouldn't it be great if the stores would allow free shopping once in a while? It'd be a miracle!* Dotty grinned at the thought.

When Dotty arrived home, her mother was still at work. Sometimes she brought back cooked food from The Martin Family Restaurant, bought at discount—a fringe benefit for working there.

As soon as Dotty entered her bedroom, she knew somebody had been there. Bruce? The scatter rug near her bookcase was crooked. Like Gloria, her magazines and books, games and stuffed animals were lined up on the shelves of her bookcase. Her newest possession was a slim box of 12 soft pastels. Where was it?

She found the pastels hidden beneath her puzzles. Opening the lid, she let out a gasp. Every stick broken!

She could hear the radio playing in her brother's room. Furious, she barged in without knocking. Bruce was sitting on his bed, reading a comic book.

"What happened to my pastels?" Dotty demanded, holding out the box.

"They dropped," he mumbled.

"What do you mean, they dropped! *You* dropped them!" Dotty shrieked. "Look at them— every stick broken! And they're almost brand new! I had to save up for weeks to buy them."

"I just wanted to try them out."

"Why didn't you wait to ask my permission?"

"You wouldn't have let me use them, and you know it!"

A blind fury exploded in Dotty. Dropping the box on the bed, she grabbed her brother by the hair and pulled him to his feet. He hollered and started swinging at her. She pulled as hard as she could, making him scream. He punched her shoulder, but she wouldn't let go. They fell to the floor, tearing at each other.

"Good heavens! What's going on here? Stop it this minute!" Their mother's voice brought the fight to a sudden halt. They scrambled to their feet, their faces flushed with rage. The brown hair on top of Bruce's head stuck up like an upside-down whiskbroom.

"Dorothy, you're acting like a four-year-old!" her mother scolded. "What's the matter with you?"

Tears welled up in Dotty's eyes. "Look what he did!" she cried, pointing to her chalks. "They cost me $6.95 plus tax, and now they're all busted!"

"You act like I did it on purpose," Bruce whined.

"Didn't you go into my room on purpose? How

dare you help yourself to my things! Do I touch your stuff?"

"All right, you've made your point," her mother said. And to Bruce, "From now until you've paid for the chalks, your allowance goes to your sister. Understand?"

"But that'll take almost four weeks!"

"Maybe it'll teach you a lesson," Dotty said self-righteously. "Hand over your two dollars."

"I spent 30 cents."

"So give me the rest."

Bruce got the money out of his drawer and plunked it into Dotty's outstretched hand. "I didn't mean to break your old chalks!"

"Never mind the excuses. Next time, stay out of my room, you hear?"

Bruce stuck out his bottom lip. He shuffled his feet. Then he sighed and asked his mother, "Can I have the broken chalks since I'm paying for them?"

"After they're paid for, yes. And no television today for either of you—for fighting."

Dotty shot a dagger glance at her brother. She had planned to watch a special for teenagers that night. Grabbing her box of pastels, she ran out of the room. *Brat!* He'd spoiled her perfect day.

That night, still seething, she deliberately disobeyed her mother. After the family was asleep, she sneaked downstairs and watched a late movie with the volume on low. She ignored her conscience. The film was an exciting mystery and she enjoyed it. She went to bed feeling smug at having put one over on her parents.

She felt tired when she got up the next morning and was still angry at Bruce. She was quiet at breakfast, and her father had to coax a smile out of her. At school she congratulated Gloria for not having a kid brother.

"Mine ticks me off," she complained, and told her friend what had happened. She added, "Last week Millie Mancini admired my butterfly pin, and you know what? Bruce told her I found it in a garbage can!"

"And did you?"

"Well . . . yes. But did he have to tell?"

Gloria laughed. Dotty didn't think it was funny. "You wouldn't laugh if it happened to you."

"Maybe not," Gloria admitted. "Still, do you think it's fun being an only child? It gets a little lonesome sometimes. I wouldn't mind having a brother."

"You want Bruce? Take him! Please!"

"Well, he's better than nothing. Ask your parents for me, will you, Dotty?"

That brought on the giggles and they both cheered up.

At noon in the cafeteria, while the monitor's back was turned, a clown named Charlie pulled Randy's chair out from under him as he sat down. Some of the kids snickered when Randy went sprawling. Dotty and Gloria were at a nearby table and saw it happen. To Charlie everything was funny, and Dotty felt like swatting him as he grinned his crocodile grin.

Getting up, Randy looked at Charlie and said, "Would you like to try that again so I can fall gracefully?"

It took Charlie by surprise, and he couldn't think of a comeback. The other boys guffawed. Randy kept a straight face and sat down to eat his lunch.

"He didn't even get mad!" said Gloria.

Randy's a good Christian, thought Dotty. He

belonged to her church, and she wondered what he'd think of her had he seen her go wild over her broken pastels. She could feel her cheeks grow hot at the thought.

5
Crazy Fun

"Let's hurry and eat. I want to try something," Gloria whispered.

"Try what?" Dotty asked her.

"Tell you in the girls' room."

They left the lunchroom early and had the washroom to themselves. Gloria withdrew a tissue from her pocket. Wrapped in it were two cigarettes, slightly bent, and a book of matches.

"One of the guys slipped them to me," she said. "My father smokes a pipe, but my mother doesn't smoke at all. I've been wondering what it's like to smoke a cigarette. It looks so elegant on TV. And so easy. You game?"

This was another "Don't," thought Dotty. Don't do this and don't do that. Defiantly, she accepted one of the cigarettes and stuck it between her lips. Gloria lighted them both. They began puffing energetically.

Dotty's face contorted as she gagged.

"Aaack!" cried Gloria, pulling the cigarette out of her mouth and going into a coughing spasm.

They coughed. And choked. And coughed some more.

As soon as they could catch their breath, they flushed the cigarettes down the toilet. They ran to the open window and stood gulping the fresh air.

"Oh, wow!" said Gloria. "What did we do wrong? They never do that on TV."

"Maybe we puffed too hard. Yuk!" Dotty made a horrible face.

"I hope the smell goes away," said Gloria. "Let's scram before somebody comes."

They beat it out of there fast and went outdoors. Sitting down on the side entrance step, they looked at each other and cracked up. When the bell rang, they giggled all the way to Room 14.

After school, Gloria withdrew a copy of *Sev-*

enteen from her bookbag. Opening the magazine, she showed Dotty what she'd hidden between the pages. "I found it in our attic."

"What is it?" Dotty stared at the long hollow metal tube. It was the size of a big straw and had what looked like a wooden mouthpiece at one end.

"It's a blowgun, dummy. A peashooter."

"Oh. Yeah. I never saw one before."

"I guess it's an old-fashioned kind of toy. You can blow dried peas and small beans through it. I've been practicing."

"Isn't it dangerous?" Dotty asked. "I mean, if it ever hit an eye."

"You gotta watch where you aim, of course. Let's have some fun with it at the mall. I brought a little bag of dried white beans. We can sit on a bench and take turns shooting at the boys walking by. When they glance around to see who did it, we'll be looking at the magazine, innocent as lambs. You game?"

Dotty laughed. "Hey, Gloria, you're kinda wild today." Actually, it did sound like fun. And dried beans couldn't hurt anybody unless you aimed at faces. "Okay, I'm game," she said. "And let's practice spelling on the way. We've got a spelldown coming up tomorrow afternoon. I think I know all the words."

At the shopping center, Gloria selected a bench which stood between The Game Room and Carvel's. Kids always gathered in that part of the mall after school. The Game Room was a hangout, mostly for teenagers. Gloria couldn't have chosen a better site for potshots.

She laid the open *Seventeen* face down on her blue-jeaned lap and discreetly slipped the peashooter and little bag of beans under it.

"Sit close to me, Dotty," she said in a low voice. "I'll stand the magazine on my lap as if we're both looking at the pictures. It'll hide the blowgun from people walking by in front of us," Gloria giggled, then quickly raised a hand to cover her mouth. "Mustn't laugh when we hit a target, or it'll give us away. Can you keep a straight face?"

"Hope so," said Dotty. And promptly tittered.

"Tell you what. Let's be Anita and Dawn again. This time we're actors. We're doing a screen test—get it?"

"Oh, I love to act," said Dotty. "Last year I had a good part in a school play. My parents said I did great. Wish you'd been around to see me."

"Good for you. Glad you told me, Anita. I'm not bad at acting myself." Glancing about, "Dawn" lowered her voice and said, "Here come two boys from one direction and a boy from the other direction. If they pass each other in front of us, watch me go to work. Now, help me hold the magazine."

The boys did pass each other. Quicky, "Dawn" aimed the peashooter at the lone boy and blew hard. Her aim was perfect. His hand slapped at the back of his neck and he whirled to look behind him.

"Look at the hairdo on this page, Anita," "Dawn" exclaimed in a clear, carrying voice. They put their heads together over the magazine, which hid their weapon from view.

"Oh, it's darling; I love it!" said "Anita." She glanced up casually at the boy, who was rubbing his neck. His gaze was on the older guys who had passed him and were now entering The Game Room. Catching "Anita's" eye, he shrugged and moved on. The girls grinned at each other, pressing their lips together to keep from giggling while the kid was within earshot.

They spent half an hour on the bench, taking potshots at guys. "Anita's" aim was poor from lack of practice. She connected only on backs. "Dawn" was able to hit arms and necks, which were more sensitive.

An elderly lady saw what they were doing. She shook her finger at them and tsk-tsked reproach-fully. They smothered their giggles as she went by.

When "Dawn" tried the trick on a grownup, he got wise to them. Walking over to the girls, he jerked the magazine off Dawn's lap, exposing the peashooter and ammunition. He glanced from her to "Anita" and said, "Don't you young ladies have anything better to do with your time?" He walked away, shaking his head.

By then the girls were tired of the game and decided to go home. It had been fun watching the expressions on their victims' faces. They'd fooled them all, except the man. "Anita" and "Dawn" had passed their screen test.

"We'll play a different game next time," said Gloria.

"Like what?" asked Dotty, knowing full well what the answer would be.

"Wait and see."

6
Too Good
to Be True

The next morning Dotty passed Andrea Tyson in the school hall and replied to her greeting with a tight "Hi."

Andrea was the smartest girl in Dotty's sixth-grade class, and the prettiest. She had shiny black hair and big, dark eyes with lashes like tiny fans. She was also kind and helpful. And rich. Her clothes were expensive, her manners gracious, her voice soft. She had just turned 12, but seemed more mature than other kids her age. A perfect little lady in every way. *Sickening!* thought Dotty.

"She's too good to be true," she remarked to Gloria, who felt the same way about Andrea.

"You're telling me. Nobody's that perfect," Gloria agreed. "Her father's vice-president of a bank, isn't he? In novels, rich girls like Andrea are usually spoiled rotten. She knows how to put her best foot forward in school so the kids will like her, but she's no better than the rest of us. Just richer."

Ignoring the envy in Gloria's voice, Dotty said, "I think I'll keep an eye on her. I bet my temper is no worse than hers. I wonder if she swears when she gets mad." *That's one thing I don't do,* she thought self-righteously.

"The way to find out is to get her mad," said Gloria with a mischievous gleam in her eye. "I think I'll sit next to her in the cafeteria this noon."

"What are you going to do?"

"Oh, I'll think of something."

Usually certain groups ate lunch together. Andrea looked surprised when Gloria grabbed a seat next to her and Dotty sat down across from her.

"You don't mind if we sit here, do you?" Gloria asked. Andrea shook her head and smiled uncertainly.

49

Watching her out of the corner of her eye, Dotty saw her bow her head and close her eyes. She was saying grace, making no attempt to hide it. Her head remained bowed for at least a half-minute. It made Dotty uncomfortable. She, too, always said grace before eating, but quickly, without the bowed head and closed eyes, so that no one would know.

She wondered what Gloria intended to do. She soon found out when her friend accidently-on-purpose knocked over her full carton of milk so that it splattered Andrea's blouse and skirt. Andrea pushed back her chair and jumped to her feet, mopping at herself with her paper napkin.

"I'm so sorry!" Gloria wiped at the table with her own napkin. "I spoiled part of your lunch, too. How clumsy of me."

"I have to agree," said Andrea. Then, taking a deep breath, she said, "It's okay, Gloria. I have a smock in my locker that I can put on. Excuse me."

Gloria raised a questioning eyebrow at Dotty, as if to say, "Is she for real?"

Does Andrea really believe the milk spilled by accident? Dotty wondered. *She must know Gloria and I aren't crazy about her. Accident or not, if it had happened to me I'd be real upset over it. I don't see how she can be so nice about it.*

Andrea returned wearing a pretty floral smock and carrying a handful of paper towels. After cleaning up the mess, she bought herself a salad and sat down with it.

Impulsively, Dotty asked her, "Aren't you even a little bit angry?" Adding, with a quick glance at Gloria, "Even though it was an accident?"

"I was upset at first," Andrea admitted.

Avoiding Gloria's eyes, Dotty persisted, "Suppose somebody did that to you on purpose? That would make you mad, wouldn't it?"

"It'd make *me* mad," spoke up one of the girls at the table.

"I'd blow my top," said another.

"I'd get even," somebody else piped up.

"Get even? Oh, no," Andrea replied. "I suppose I could, but Jesus helps me love and forgive when it's needed."

A hush fell over the table. Dotty squirmed uncomfortably.

Andrea glanced around at the faces turned toward her. Clearing her throat, she said, "Before coming here I attended a private school. That's why you girls don't know what a brat I used to be. When I couldn't get my own way, I'd have a tantrum—and it usually worked. I got everything I wanted, including a pony. But you know something? I wasn't happy."

"Why not, if you had everything you wanted?" somebody asked.

"I guess I didn't like myself much. But after I came to know Jesus, He helped me to change. He's really neat." Andrea's smile lit up her whole face.

A girl at the end of the table whispered something to her companion. They looked at Andrea sideways and giggled behind their hands. But the other girls seemed impressed by her frankness and interested in what she was saying.

"In what way did God help you change?" a girl asked.

"Well—the selfishness. Control of temper. And I'm learning from the Bible what love is really all about." Andrea picked up a forkful of salad. "I like myself much better now." She added with a smile, "But God isn't finished with me yet."

What guts—to witness like that in front of

everybody, thought Dotty. She stared at Andrea and the thought came to her, *Now I'm not even sure I'm a Christian.*

Not a Christian? Of course she was a Christian! Hadn't she been raised in the church by Christian parents? Hadn't she always believed in Christ as her Savior? Didn't she attend worship services regularly and tithe out of her allowance?

Resentment toward Andrea surged within Dotty. If it weren't for her, she wouldn't be having these doubts. The guiltier she felt, the angrier she became.

As they returned to their classroom, Gloria said, "From what Andrea told us, she's become a goody-goody Christian. I bet she thinks she's just about perfect now."

No, thought Dotty; *she told us God isn't finished with her yet.* Dotty didn't say it aloud, for she was in no mood to defend Andrea Tyson.

Miss Brent, the prettiest teacher in Lincoln Elementary School, was well-liked by her students in Room 14. She always tried to think of ways to make schoolwork fun. Today she lined up everybody in two rows, one on each side of the classroom, for a spelldown.

"I hope you've studied your words for this," she said. "It will help in your final exams."

Dotty enjoyed spelldowns. She usually did well and had won a couple of times. Right now, however, she felt nervous and upset. She tried to calm down, for she wanted to win.

The teacher held up a prize ribbon. "The one who remains standing gets the blue ribbon," she said, smiling. "It'll make the spelldown more fun."

She began giving out the words. Each time Dotty's turn came, she pronounced the word carefully, then spelled it correctly. A few of the students obviously hadn't studied. They went down quickly. The rest stayed up for a good while, and the spelldown lasted longer than usual.

Finally, all were seated except Dotty, Andrea, and Randy. Dotty was standing across the room from her competitors. Randy looked solemn. Andrea seemed relaxed and confident. Dotty, lips tightening, glanced away. *That girl has everything—looks, clothes, money, personality, lots of friends—and she's a good speller besides. It's just too much!*

"Dorothy, it's your turn," she heard the teacher say. "Shall I repeat the word?"

Dotty swallowed. "I . . . I'm sorry, Miss Brent, I didn't hear it."

Her word was "congratulate." Dotty repeated it and spelled it. As soon as she had finished she knew she'd made a mistake. She had used a *d* instead of a *t*. But once you completed a word, you could not go back and do it over.

Andrea had her chance next and got it right. Dotty walked to her seat with her head down. She knew she shouldn't have missed that word. All because she'd been thinking about Andrea!

It was Randy's turn again with "exercise." Dotty hoped he'd win the spelldown, now that she was out of it. He lost, using a *z* instead of an *s*. Andrea got it right and won the blue ribbon. Miss Brent congratulated her, and so did Randy. The class applauded—all but Dotty and Gloria.

I hate her, thought Dotty. She knew it was wrong to hate, but at the moment she couldn't care less.

7
More Mischief

That afternoon, Dotty went bike riding with Gloria. Although they both had other casual friends, they preferred each other's company. Dotty admired Gloria's daredevil spunk, even though it disturbed her at times. One thing about Gloria, she was never dull.

Gloria led the bike ride to an apartment building, got off, and led Dotty into the foyer.

"Are we going to visit somebody?" Dotty asked.

"No, we're just gonna have some fun. You can't

get past this foyer unless somebody pushes a button in their apartment to unlock the door. I'll ring all the doorbells on this side. You do the same on the opposite wall. When the door starts buzzing, we'll scram."

It seemed a harmless prank. Dotty followed Gloria's lead. Between them, they rang a dozen doorbells. Responses started almost immediately—buzz . . . buzz . . . buzz. . . . Giggling, the girls took off.

Gloria led the way to a wide, smoothly paved road in a well-to-do section of town where there wasn't much traffic. Dotty looked around.

"I've never been on this street before. What pretty houses."

"I've only been here once myself," said Gloria.

"Rich people live in this area, huh? Look at that yellow stucco house across the street down there," Dotty pointed. "It looks Spanish, with that red tile roof and all those arches and fancy black grillwork. Look at the fountain and the pansies lining the walk. Pretty."

"I remembered how long and smooth this road is," Gloria told her. "That's why we came—to have a bike race. We both have 10-speed bicycles, so

58

we're evenly matched. We'll go the length of this street, okay? And the loser has to do whatever the winner commands."

"Like, if I win and command you to do a song and dance act right on the sidewalk, you've gotta do it?" Dotty asked with a giggle.

Gloria grinned at her. "If you win, your wish is my command. You game?"

"Sounds fun. But *please* don't ask me to sing and dance on the street. Anything but that."

"I've got something else in mind. Get ready . . . on your mark . . . *go!*"

They raced down the street, remaining neck-to-neck most of the way. But then, with a sudden burst of speed, Gloria pulled ahead. She won the race. It was fun, no matter who won, and they laughed breathlessly. Flipping down their kick-stands, they sat on the curb to rest.

"What are you gonna make me do?" Dotty wanted to know.

"We'll just ride our bikes and whatever I do, you copy me. If I go slow, you go slow. If I speed up, you speed up. I'll think of other things on the way. You just follow the leader."

"Sounds easy enough."

"If I cut across somebody's lawn, you've gotta follow right on my tail, Dotty, hear? Something daring will make the game exciting."

"Suppose somebody looks out their window while we're on their property?"

"So what? Nobody around here knows us. We'll just scram away fast. That's the fun of it, see?"

"So lead on," Dotty said recklessly.

Gloria started out slow and easy. She increased her speed. She slowed down again. "Watch me, I'm drunk," she announced over her shoulder, and began zigzagging her bicycle. Dotty chuckled and did likewise. When they tired of that, they made circles in the middle of the road, waved to some children, and went forward again.

Suddenly Gloria cut into a yard, circled a tree, and rode across the driveway. Dotty followed close behind. As they rode across the rest of the lawn, somebody banged on one of the windows at them. They took off, laughing.

They rode up another driveway and down again. With a gleam in her eye, Gloria said, "The next stunt will be the last."

They were now in front of the Spanish-style

house, where the walk was lined with colorful pansies. Gloria turned in and drove her bike along one side of the walk and down the other side, crushing the blossoms beneath her wheels. Dotty unplugged her conscience and followed the leader.

A youthful voice shouted, "Hey, what are you doing? Stop that! Stop it! How could you be so mean!"

The girls glanced over their shoulders as they pedaled away. Dotty was surprised to see Andrea standing by the front door. Her hands were clenched and her face was red with anger.

"Well, what do you know! It's the Tyson house," Gloria exclaimed. "And this time we got Andrea mad for sure, ha ha!"

Somehow, Dotty didn't feel like laughing.

As she tried to concentrate on her homework that evening, Dotty kept remembering what she and Gloria had done. There'd been no satisfaction for her in making Andrea lose her temper. Andrea had a right to be angry. Even so, she hadn't used bad language or called them names. Dotty knew that if somebody deliberately destroyed the flowers in *her* yard, she'd be furious. She might not swear, but she wasn't beyond name-calling.

Somebody had lovingly cared for those pansies, she thought regretfully—and trampling them was a rotten thing to do. Why had she followed the leader like a dumb sheep? Now she was guilty of vandalism, and it was weighing heavily on her heart. If only she could turn back the clock. How was she going to face Andrea at school tomorrow?

Swallowing, she whispered, "I'm sorry, God. Please forgive me."

First go and be reconciled to your brother. The portion of Scripture was like a flashcard in Dotty's mind. She could see it and recognized it as part of the Sermon on the Mount. It was as if Jesus were speaking to her directly, and it meant she had to ask forgiveness of the Tysons.

When she finally finished her homework, Dotty went to the family room for something to read. A book was lying on the table. She glanced at the title: *Walk in His Steps and Other True Stories*.

Lifting the cover, Dotty saw the name and address of her church stamped inside. Her mother must have borrowed the book from the church library. She carried it into the kitchen where Mrs. Russell was polishing silver.

"May I take this book to my room, Mom? Are you finished with it?"

"No, but go ahead. They're family stories for all ages. Is your homework done?"

"All done. I'm gonna put on my pajamas and read in bed."

Her mother smiled at her. "I used to love to do that when I was young. I'd take a snack to bed with me and read myself to sleep. I can still remember how cozy-comfy I felt, eating and reading. Especially in a nice warm bed on a cold winter's night."

"I know what you mean," Dotty said, filling a paper cup from a can of mixed nuts.

When she had made herself comfortable on her bed, she bit into a brazil nut and turned to the first story in her book. The beginning riveted her attention at once, for it reminded her of herself. It was written in the first person by a teenaged girl named Mabel. It told about yelling at her younger brother for spilling water on one of her paintings. A shouting match followed, until the mother broke it up. As Mabel confessed other failings in her story, Dotty was able to identify with her anger, her problems, her rebellion. Disliking herself and wanting to change, Mabel, a lukewarm Christian, decided to follow in Christ's footsteps by asking herself before she did anything, "What would *He* do?" With God's help, she found it made a real difference in her life.

By the time Dotty finished the true account, she was totally convinced of her sins. The anger over Bruce, the rebellion concerning Sunday school, her jealousy over Andrea—all slipped from her like a discarded dress that no longer appealed. She thought of Jesus, on the cross, giving His all because of sin—her sins included. *How can He care so much for me when I've been so thoughtless of— no, spiteful toward—others? Oh, Jesus—I'm so sorry! Forgive me—please! Lord, be merciful to me, a sinner.*

Forgiveness washed over her in a cleansing wave, and she buried her head in her pillow to stifle her sobs. How could she have been so petty, so selfish and unloving?

When the storm of weeping subsided, Dotty knelt by her bed thankful for God's forgiveness for all the wrong she had done. She wondered how much difference it would make in her life if she tried to be more like Jesus and follow in His footsteps. Would He help her the way He had helped Andrea and Mabel? She wanted to promise Him she'd do it—but suppose she couldn't keep it up? She'd hate to make God a promise and end up breaking her word. But she couldn't get it out of her mind. Finally, she bowed her head and vowed to do her best to follow Christ, at least until the end of the month. That didn't seem too difficult, and she felt really good about it.

Slipping out of bed, Dotty went to speak to her brother. He was sitting at his desk in his room. "Bruce, I'm sorry I pulled your hair the other day. Forgive me?"

"Well . . . okay," he said, adding, "My head's still sore, you know. Man, can you pull hair!"

Dotty had to smile. "I'm never going to pull your hair again. I may bite or kick you," she teased, "but I won't pull hair."

"Hey, that's big of you," said Bruce, and they both laughed.

Dotty went back to her room smiling.

But then she remembered she still had to face Andrea in the morning.

8
A New Beginning

Facing Andrea was one of the most difficult things Dotty ever had to do. As she walked toward the locker where Andrea was hanging her smock, Dotty could feel a fire rising in her cheeks. Her whole head felt on fire—she was that ashamed. She wanted to turn and run out of the building, but what good would that do? She'd have to come back sooner or later. Besides, she knew what God expected of her.

Andrea's expression was grave as Dotty paused beside her.

"Andrea, I . . . " Dotty couldn't meet the girl's eyes as she put up a hand to her crimson face. "Would you forgive me, please, for messing up the pansies?" she asked in a small, tremulous voice. "I didn't know that was your house—not that that makes any difference. I'm so sorry. I've never done anything like that before. I asked God to forgive me, and I hope you will, too. And maybe I should apologize to your parents as well. They might like me to do some work around the yard to make up for what I did."

Having said all that, Dotty glanced up into Andrea's brown eyes—soft, gentle eyes.

"Of course, I forgive you, Dorothy. I planted and cared for the pansies myself, so you don't have to talk to my parents. And the flowers probably wouldn't have lasted much longer anyway. But I'm really glad you spoke to me about it."

Dotty's eyes grew moist. How kind Andrea was! And what a load off her heart! She felt so much better now.

"Thanks," she said huskily, "thanks a lot." She started toward Room 14, then turned back. "Andrea? My friends call me Dotty."

"Sure, Dotty."

67

They smiled at each other.

Dotty felt so good after that, so lighthearted, that she could hardly believe it. She ate lunch with Gloria as usual, but turned down an invitation to go bike riding again. On her way out of the lunchroom, she paused to tousle her brother's hair, thinking he was going to be a handsome guy one day.

"Hey, cut it out." Bruce ducked his head self-consciously, but he was grinning. It was seldom that his sister paid attention to him at school.

When Dotty got home she found a note from her mother. It read:

Dotty,

I forgot to tell you this morning that I promised to visit a sick friend (Mrs. Daniels) after work today. I'll be late getting home. Please scrub some potatoes for baking and get them in the oven before five. I was going to make meatloaf, but instead I'll broil quick hamburger patties.

Thanks,

Mom

Dotty decided she could manage the meatloaf herself, although she'd never made one. Washing her hands, she went to work. She mixed the lean ground beef with the ingredients she had seen her mother use. She didn't know exactly how much to put in, but by tasting as she went along, she managed very well. She decided to add garlic powder for extra flavor, her own personal touch. The mixture had good consistency and shaped up fine into a loaf. Dotty was happy as she put four big potatoes in the preheated oven, later followed by the meatloaf.

She sliced a cucumber and two tomatoes into a salad bowl. The lettuce she tore with her fingers, remembering that her mother had once told her that cutting lettuce with a knife made the edges turn brown if prepared ahead of time. She covered the bowl with transparent wrap and placed it in the refrigerator. All her mother had to do was add the dressing and mix.

When she walked in, the table was set and dinner was almost ready. It smelled delicious. Mrs. Russell was so surprised she pretended to swoon.

"I don't believe it!" she said. "Dotty, how wonderful. Thank you, dear." She gave her a hug. "Is Bruce home?"

"He's upstairs. And maybe you should taste

my meatloaf before you thank me," Dotty said with a grin.

Her father arrived home shortly. As they set the food on the table, Dotty caught her mother's eye and put her finger to her lips. She whispered in her brother's ear. He nodded. They were not to mention who had made the meatloaf until the man of the house had tasted it.

When he did, he smiled and said to his wife, "Ah, so you finally decided to try the garlic, eh? Didn't I tell you it would improve the flavor?"

The others laughed, and Dotty proudly announced that it was she who had made the dinner. Her mother promised to add garlic to her meatloaf in the future.

It rained on Saturday. Dotty agreed to play Scrabble with Bruce after they'd done their chores, even though she would rather have curled up with a book. When they paused for a snack, she offered him the last cookie instead of grabbing it for herself as she usually did. But when her brother spilled milk on the floor, she started to yell at him. Catching herself, she mumbled an apology and helped him clean the mess with paper towels. Bruce didn't say anything; he just looked puzzled.

In the school cafeteria on Monday, Dotty saw Joan Nelson sitting by herself and suddenly felt sympathy for her. Joan was a fat, grumpy girl who was good at starting arguments. The kids avoided her, and Gloria couldn't stand her. But with her new way of looking at people, through the eyes of Jesus, Dotty sensed that Joan must be lonely.

Going over to her table, she sat next to her with a cheery "Hi, Joan." Joan's eyebrows went up, but Dotty pretended not to notice. Although Gloria was scowling at her, she waved for her to join them. Her friend tossed her head and deliberately turned her back.

Dotty shrugged and smiled at Joan. To get a conversation rolling, she began asking friendly questions. Was Joan nervous about the final exams coming up in a few days? Was she planning anything special for the summer? Did she have a pet?

Dotty shared half her banana with her and told her about making a great meatloaf on her first try. Joan then confided that she loved to cook and

71

wanted to be a chef someday. Before the lunch period was over, Dotty could tell the girl was beginning to warm up to her. She was determined not to ignore Joan in the future, and regretted she hadn't tried being nice to her before.

Trying to follow Jesus wasn't always a happy thing, however. Gloria was angry at her for leaving her to go sit with Joan. When Dotty tried to explain her new attitude, Gloria accused her of being "holier than thou" and flounced away, refusing to listen. It put a damper on Dotty's day.

She arrived home from school before Bruce and was in the family room when he came in.

"I'm going to the park playground. Be home before dinner," he said, aiming a school book in the general direction of a chair. It missed. He ran out without bothering to pick it up. Ordinarily, Dotty would have shouted, "Come back here!" This time she merely sighed and picked up the book herself.

As she settled down to study, she wondered if Gloria was still her friend.

9
Gladness—
and Sadness

Dotty arrived at school early on Tuesday. Andrea was early, too, and they entered the building together.

"Dotty, would you like to go to Carvel's for a double cone after school?" Andrea asked. "My treat."

"Oh, that would be nice." The invitation surprised and pleased Dotty. Perhaps she and Andrea could become good friends.

Gloria arrived as they were talking in the hall. She stared at them sullenly. Dotty excused herself and walked over to her. "Are you still mad at me for sitting with Joan yesterday at lunch?

"I thought we were best friends," Gloria snapped.

"Are we? How could I know that, the way you act at times."

Gloria pouted. "I was going to ask you to go to the mall with me after school today."

"Not today. Andrea asked me first. She's treating me to ice cream. I'll go with you another time, okay?"

"Yeah. Sure." Gloria turned away and left her abruptly.

Catching her lower lip between her teeth, Dotty slowly walked toward her classroom. What was the matter with Gloria? She seemed a different girl from the one she'd made friends with some months before. How could they go on being friends if she continued acting this way?

She had lunch with her, as usual, but Gloria was sullen and withdrawn and hardly spoke.

On the way to the mall, Dotty shyly confided to Andrea about wanting to follow Jesus Christ. Andrea seemed happy for her. She told her it wouldn't always be easy, but that Christ's love and help from the Holy Spirit would see her through.

"But I can't be perfect like Jesus was," Dotty worried.

"Who can? We'll never be perfect till we get to heaven. And don't expect to change your ways all at once. I was still bratty for a while, you know," Andrea told her. "But I became very self-conscious about it. My sense of right and wrong sharpened, and it bothered me when I behaved badly. My mom says, that was the Holy Spirit convicting me, making me sensitive to sin and to other people's feelings. She and Dad have become Christians, too. I still get mad once in a while, but not like before."

"I'm reading my Bible," Dotty said. "I feel like I'm getting to know the Lord in a different way than before. Better. Closer. You know?"

"I know. A personal relationship," Andrea said, smiling. "And you know something? I find I do best when I take things one day at a time, like Jesus said we should do. Hey, what's your favorite ice cream flavor?"

"Strawberry."

"Mine's chocolate. I lo-o-ove chocolate. Can't wait to have some. Beat you to the mall!"

They arrived giggly and out of breath. The double cones they ordered were well stacked, and they thoroughly enjoyed them as they strolled around the mall.

"That was yummy," Dotty said as she swallowed the last morsel of crispy cone. "Thanks, Andrea."

"You're welcome. Let's go to Woolworth's. I want a pack of gum."

They rounded the corner of the candy aisle just in time to see a young girl pick up a package of candies. She was about to slip it into her book bag, when she looked up and saw them staring at her. Her hand faltered. Her face flushed. Replacing the package, she turned and hurried away toward the door. The girl was Gloria.

Dotty and Andrea exchanged shocked glances. Neither spoke. Andrea selected a pack of spearmint gum, paid for it, and they left the store. They had to part outside, as each lived in a different direction. Dotty accepted a stick of gum from her new friend and asked helplessly, "What can I do?"

Andrea knew she was referring to Gloria. "Go on being her friend. Try to talk to her about it. And pray for her. I will, too."

Dotty swallowed hard and nodded.

"Sometime in July I'm going to have a pajama party at my house," Andrea told her. "I hope you'll come. I'd like us to be friends."

"I'd love to come. And to be friends with you, Andrea. I think you're super. Thanks again. I'll see you tomorrow."

Dotty walked away from the mall with mixed feelings—gladness that Andrea wanted her for a friend, sadness over Gloria. Should she try to talk to Gloria immediately? Before her parents got home from work? She felt reluctant to do so, embarrassed, and her feet dragged. Yet she knew they needed to talk. Not just about the candy incident, but Gloria's whole attitude. She had said she thought Dotty was her best friend. Then why did she flare up at her for the least little thing? If she had a problem, why couldn't she share it with her? Wasn't that what friends were for? And why had she stooped to stealing?

Turning her steps in the direction of Gloria's house, Dotty still felt the shock of observing her friend in the act of shoplifting. When they did it with paper dolls, it was just a game. Or was it? Was Gloria planning even then to do it for real?

Would she have tried to persuade Dotty to shoplift also if they'd gone to the mall together today?

Dotty shuddered. How easy it was to fall into sin! You started with mischief like shooting beans at kids, knocking over milk cartons, ringing door-bells, riding bikes over lawns. Then came deliberate destruction of flowers. And now stealing. What next?

Upon opening her door to Dotty's ring, Gloria scowled at her. "What do you want?" she demanded belligerently.

"I . . . I . . . oh, Gloria, why did you do it?"

"I don't know why. And it's none of your business!"

"But suppose you'd gotten caught?"

"Today was the first time anybody saw me."

Dotty's mouth fell open. Gloria had done it before!

"It would serve my father right if I got caught! Oh, boy, wouldn't he like the trouble that would cause? That would show him!"

"You're talking crazy!" Dotty gasped. "Look, can I come in?"

"No! Go back to your new friend!" Gloria was crying now. "My father found somebody new, too.

79

He doesn't live here anymore. He doesn't love my mother and me, or he wouldn't have left us. He's getting a divorce!"

The door slammed shut.

10
One Day at a Time

Despite having the door shut in her face, Dotty could feel Gloria's pain. *A divorce!*

She walked home slowly, head lowered. So this was what had been affecting Gloria's behavior. Had she kept it to herself out of shame? And why should she think her father didn't love her anymore? He was divorcing his wife, not his daughter. Poor Gloria. She was hurting badly. And Mrs. Powell. Perhaps it was risky to marry a man who looked like a movie star. There were always girls running after movie stars.

I couldn't stand it if this was happening to my family. I love my Dad, but I think I'd hate him if he left Mom for another woman. I'd still love him, I guess, but I'd hate him too. At least for a while.

Dotty sighed as she reached home. She must put Gloria out of her mind for now. Tomorrow was Wednesday, and final exams started on Thursday. She had to concentrate on her studies.

The next day, she fell into step with Gloria on their way to the cafeteria. "I'm sorry about what's happening to your family, Gloria," she said. "And I'm still your friend, you know. Just because I've made a new friend doesn't mean you and I are quits. When you feel like it, we'll get together. Okay?"

Gloria did not speak, but her expression softened a little. Dotty laid a hand on her arm. "We've got only two half days of school left. Will you phone me after that? Anytime. Will you let me prove I'm your friend?"

Slowly, Gloria inclined her head. Seeing her chin quiver, Dotty put an arm around her waist.

"We're leaving next week to visit my grandparents in Buffalo," Gloria said. "My mom wants to get away. We'll be gone two weeks."

"What about Pixie?"

"We're taking her with us."

"Well, call me when you get back."

Gloria was quiet during lunch and merely picked at her food, but Dotty felt she was lending support just by being with her.

When school let out Friday noon after the last of the exams, Dotty felt sure she had passed all her subjects. She would miss dear Miss Brent, but the thought of moving up to junior high school excited her. Meanwhile, she had the whole summer before her.

Bruce also felt he'd be promoted, although he didn't expect a high grade in English. As they fixed peanut butter and jelly sandwiches for lunch, Dotty offered to help him if he still had trouble with English in the sixth grade.

"It's one of my favorite subjects," she told him. "I'll be able to help you if you get stuck."

Her brother eyed her with suspicion. "How come the offer? You were never too keen about helping me before. You usually had something more important to do—or so you said."

"I helped you sometimes, didn't I?"

"Not too willingly, as I remember."

"Well, that was then and this is now."

Dotty wasn't ready to tell her family that she was trying to live as Jesus would. There were a lot of days left in June, and she was still afraid of failing—even though Andrea had told her no Christian could expect to be perfect. She felt as though her faith was still shaky, yet her love for Christ was growing steadily as she read about Him daily in her Bible. Her mind still wandered in church, but not as much as previously. She still wasn't crazy about the way Mrs. Courtney taught Sunday school, but she did try to be more accepting and cooperative.

Impatience was still a problem with Dotty. Now that she wanted to be a better person, a good Christian, she wanted it to happen quickly. *I guess I want too much too soon. I'd better try living one day at a time, like Jesus said. Maybe that'll make things easier.*

"I think I'll go to the store and get a candy

bar," she said as she cleared the table. "What are you going to do, Bruce?"

"Don't know yet." He shuffled his feet. "You know, it's pretty hard going without an allowance. I haven't had a candy bar in a while."

Dotty got the hint. "Come along and I'll treat you," she offered.

"Thanks!" Bruce glanced at her sideways. "Don't suppose you'd let me use your pastels? Before I finish paying for breaking them?"

Dotty smiled as she looked at him. He was just a kid. And not all that bad a brother. She knew a girl whose kid brother was impossible, much worse than Bruce. But, then, the sister was no angel herself.

"Yes, you can use them," she said.

"Yeah? You sure? I don't want you screaming if you catch me with them."

"That was then; this is now."

"What's with this 'That was then and this is now'?"

"Bruce, just accept and don't ask questions, huh? Maybe . . . maybe we can have a talk at the end of June; I'll have things to tell you. I want to see how something works out first."

85

Meanwhile I should set good examples for him, she thought.

"Bruce, who don't we like on our block?"

"Miss Pest across the street," he replied promptly.

"Miss Best, you mean," Dotty corrected with a grin.

"Pest is more like it. Hollers if my ball goes in her yard. Hollers if we make noise playing in the street. She doesn't like kids, that grumpy old lady. All she likes is her cat."

"Suppose we pick a bouquet of flowers for her from our garden. She hardly has any in her yard. I know Mom wouldn't mind."

"You crazy? Why her?"

"You don't think it would be a nice thing to do?" Dotty persisted.

"Well, sure, but why?"

"Didn't Jesus say we should love one another, especially the unlovely?"

Bruce's brown eyes widened and his mouth snapped shut. He couldn't argue against Jesus.

Miss Best looked stunned when they presented her with a beautiful mixed bouquet. "We thought you might like having some of our flowers," Dotty said. "My brother and I picked them for you."

The old lady stammered her thanks. At a loss for words, she held the fragrant bouquet against her face. They could tell she was touched. Bruce glanced at Dotty and smiled. She could see that the giving had touched him in some way, too.

So it went—walking in the steps of Jesus, whether Dotty felt like it or not. When she succeeded, she felt great. When she failed, she asked forgiveness and tried again. She knew God would keep on helping her, step by step.

The final report cards showed that Dotty had been promoted with a B+ average, Bruce with B−. And by the time June 30th rolled around, Mr. and Mrs. Russell had noticed the change in their daughter and were more than pleased. It was obvious God was working in her life. It was also apparent that her behavior was having a good influence on her brother.

That night, while Dotty was reading the Bible in bed, Bruce knocked, then popped his head in the doorway. "You said you'd have things to tell

87

me when this month ended," he reminded her. "You've been real nice, and I'm curious. I think it has to do with that"—he pointed to her Bible— "because you've been reading it a lot lately. How come?"

Dotty smiled at him. "You really want to know?"

"Sure. Man, you've changed so much it's like a miracle!"

"You mean I'm perfect?" she kidded.

"No, but you're sure different."

"Suppose I tell you all about it tomorrow, Bruce. First, you really should read the account that inspired me to want to change. Go ask Mom for her church library book, will you? Read the very first story. Then tomorrow you'll have a better understanding of what I tell you about me."

"Okay." Bruce withdrew his head and closed the door.

Perhaps Mabel's account would inspire him also, thought Dotty. It might help him understand that it isn't enough if only your head knows that Christ is the Savior; your heart needs to know He's *your* Savior—and you should live as though He's your Savior.

Setting her Bible on the nightstand, Dotty leaned back against her pillow with a little smile on her lips. She could hardly believe it was only three weeks since she'd started on this spiritual journey. How could you feel so much older and wiser in just three weeks?

Her thoughts turned to Gloria. She needed Christ in her life also. He could help her and her mother in this terrible crisis they were going through. She would have a talk with Gloria about it and encourage her and stand by her. Andrea would be her friend, too—Dotty felt sure of it. Gloria needed friends badly right now.

Lord, thank You for helping me keep my promise. Please keep on helping me, one step at a time.